Maggie
and the Pirate

To Bonnie Keats

ISBN   0-590-42661-3

Copyright © 1979 by Ezra Jack Keats.
All rights reserved. Published by Scholastic Inc.,
730 Broadway, New York, NY 10003, by arrangement with
Macmillan Publishing Company.
Blue Ribbon is a registered trademark of Scholastic Inc.

12 11 10 9 8 7 6 5 4 3   0 1 2 3 4 5/9

Printed in the U.S.A.   08

Maggie
and the Pirate

EZRA JACK KEATS

SCHOLASTIC INC.

New York Toronto London Auckland Sydney

Maggie and her parents lived in an old bus
which they made into a home.
Maggie was feeding Niki, her pet cricket,
when her mother called from across the river.

"Maggie! Come over please! I need some things from the grocery."

"Okay, Ma, we'll be right there."

Maggie paddled home.

She hung Niki's cage on a tree next to her house.

Then she got her mother's shopping list, and was off.

"Bye, bye, Niki. Have a nice snooze," she called.

On her way she passed her friends.

"Hey, what a cage my Pop built for Niki!" she yelled.

"Wow! Are you lucky!" called Paco. "Can we see it?"

"Sure—I'll pick you up on my way home," said Maggie.

On her way back she picked up Paco and Katie.

They helped her carry the groceries home.

When they got to the tree, something was missing!

The cage and Niki were gone!

Instead there was a note.

"Pirate?" asked Katie.

"Yeah, who's the pirate?" Paco asked.

Maggie stared at the note in horror.

THE PIRATE WAS HERE

Paco and Katie tried and tried to take her mind off Niki.

But it was no use.

"I miss Niki," Maggie sighed. "And that pirate—
he won't know what to feed him—Niki might starve."

Maggie began tacking up signs.

"What's so special about a cricket anyway?"
asked Katie.

"I like him—that's what!" answered Maggie.

"I'm going to find that pirate!" shouted Maggie.

"We'll come, too," said Paco.

"But how will we know what he looks like?"

"What if he's bigger than us?" whispered Katie.

They started out.

They looked and looked.

But they couldn't find the pirate anywhere.

It was getting dark.

Her friends got tired and straggled behind.

Maggie stopped and listened.

Crickets were chirping in the night.

"I must find Niki—before it's too late!" she said.

Suddenly, she came upon a tree house
she'd never seen before.

She walked over softly,
climbed up very quietly, and peeped in.
IT WAS THE PIRATE'S HIDEOUT!
And there was the pirate holding Niki's cage!

"Hey—I know you—
and that's my cricket!"
Maggie dived into the tree house.
She scuffled with the pirate,
trying with all her strength to get Niki.

SPLASH!

The tree house came loose and crashed into the water!

Maggie sloshed around in the dark, searching for Niki.

She saw something familiar floating by.

It was the cage!

She fished it out, and opened it.

There was Niki! But he didn't move.

"Niki's dead! He drowned," Maggie cried.

She ran off with Niki, leaving the cage behind.

"Maggie," she heard her friends call.

She saw Paco and Katie.

They ran to her. "We got lost," cried Paco. "It's so dark!"

"Wow! Look at you! What happened?

Did you find Niki?" asked Katie.

Maggie opened her hand and showed them.

"Poor Niki," said Paco.

Maggie told them everything that had happened.

"And the pirate is that new kid around here," she said.

"So he's the one," whispered Katie.

They buried Niki.

Maggie wrote his name on a piece of wood
and put it over the small grave.

Paco picked some flowers and brought them over.

Then they sang sad songs.

Suddenly, the pirate appeared!

"Why did you do that?" asked Maggie.
"We never did anything to you!"
"It was the cage—
  I wanted it real bad," said the pirate.
"I didn't mean for the cricket to die.
  My ol' man—
  he never makes anything for me.
  He doesn't ever talk to me."
The pirate handed the cage to Maggie.

She held it up.

A beautiful sound came out!

She looked in.

There was a new cricket inside.

They all sat down together.

Nobody said anything.

They listened to the new cricket singing.

Crickets all around joined in.